Dreaming of Harvestar

OUT FROM BONEVILLE
TRIBUTE EDITION

BY JEFF SMITH
WITH COLOR BY STEVE HAMAKER

graphix

An Imprint of

SCHOLASTIC

This book is for Vijaya.

All rights reserved. Published by Graphix, an imprint of Scholastic Inc., *Publishers since 1920.* SCHOLASTIC, GRAPHIX, and associated logos are trademarks and/or registered trademarks of Scholastic Inc.

Library of Congress Catalog Card Number 2014946134
ISBN 978-0-545-80070-9

ACKNOWLEDGMENTS

Harvestar Family Crest designed by Charles Vess, color by Tom Gaadt
Map of *The Valley* by Mark Crilley, color by Tom Gaadt
Cover and About the Author color by Tom Gaadt

10 9 8 7 6 5 4 3 2 1   15 16 17 18 19
This edition first printing, March 2015
Book design by David Saylor and Phil Falco
Printed in the U.S.A. 23

CONTENTS

DON'T GET HIM STARTED.

THEY CAN'T **DO** THIS TO **ME!** YOU CAN'T DO ANYTHING TO A **RICH** PERSON THAT HE DOESN'T **WANT!**

GASP! OH! TH' HORRIBLE INJUSTICE OF IT ALL! I'M STILL REELING WITH SHOCK!!

I'M A RESPECTED COMMUNITY **LEADER!** A **SHINING PILLAR** OF **MORAL STRENGTH!**

... SO A COUPLE OF SHADY **BUSINESS** DEALS WENT SOUR... IS **THAT** ANY REASON TO RUN TH' MOST **BELOVED BONE** IN BONEVILLE OUT ON A **RAIL?!**

YES.

BELOVED? TH' MAYOR DECLARED A SCHOOL **HOLIDAY** JUST SO TH' KIDS COULD COME AND THROW **ROCKS** AT YOU!

INGRATES!

OH, THEY'LL **RUE** TH' DAY THEY CHASED **PHONCIBLE P. BONE** OUTTA THEIR CRUMMY OL' TOWN!

⋚ SNIFF! ⋚

NOW, NOW, LITTLE BUCKAROO! DON'T BE **SAD!** IT'S A BEAUTIFUL DAY! THERE'S NOT A **CLOUD IN TH' SKY!**

HEY--!

LEMME SEE THAT!

HERE'S YOUR PROBLEM, FONE BONE! WE'RE OFF THE **MAP!** GET A BIGGER MAP!

THAT'S AS BIG AS MAPS GET! WE'RE IN UNCHARTED TERRITORY!

WELL, GET US BACK!

I CAN'T! WE'RE LOST!

TO BOLDLY GO WHERE NO BONE HAS GONE BEFORE!

STICK A SOCK IN IT, CABBAGE HEAD!

DON'T GET ME WRONG, FONE BONE -- I'M GRATEFUL YOU WERE ABLE TO GET ME OUTTA TOWN -- BUT TELL ME ... **WHY** DID YOU HAFTA GO AN' BRING **HIM** WITH US?

TO TORTURE YOU.

I KNEW THAT!

HEY, PHONEY! BAD NEWS ... WE'RE OUT OF WATER!

THAT'S THE **LAST STRAW!**

DON'T GET MAD AT SMILEY BONE! THIS MESS ISN'T **HIS** FAULT!

THAT'S RIGHT! TH' TOWNSPEOPLE AREN'T MAD AT **US!** THEY RAN **YOU** OUTTA TOWN 'CAUSE YOU'RE A SELFISH, LITTLE **GREEDBAG!**

I CAN'T BELIEVE IT! NOT ONLY AM I **BROKE** - - NOW I'M GONNA **DIE** BROKE!

GASP! COFF! COFF!

OH, YOU'RE NOT GONNA DIE! I JUST HOPE YOU LEARNED YOUR LESSON!

WATER! I NEED **WATER!** I CAN FEEL MY TONGUE **CRACKING!**

HEY, COUSINS, LOOK WHAT I FOUND! I THINK IT'S A MAP!

?!

SURE ENOUGH! LOOK! IT'S A MAP OF THAT MOUNTAIN RANGE!

I'M **SAVED!** GIVE IT TO ME!

GIMME A DOLLAR FIRST.

WHAT?

GO ON, PHONEY! GIVE HIM A DOLLAR!

WHAT?!

WE'RE LOST IN THE MIDDLE OF TH' DESERT! GIVE HIM A DOLLAR!

PHONEY--⁎ SAY! THERE'S THAT MAP!

HUH! I WONDER IF THIS REALLY IS A MAP OF THAT MOUNTAIN RANGE... MAYBE I BETTER HANG ON TO IT!

I MIGHT NEED IT TO SAVE PHONEY BONE...

...AGAIN!

HMMF.

I'M ALWAYS GETTIN' HIM OUTTA TROUBLE!

WELL, COUSIN OR NOT... WHEN WE GET BACK TO BONEVILLE, PHONEY'S GONNA HAVE TO FACE THE MUSIC BY HIMSELF!

I'VE HAD IT! FROM NOW ON, HE CAN OUTRUN ANGRY MOBS, AN' FALL OFF CLIFFS WITHOUT MY HELP!

WHAT KIND OF A PATSY DOES HE TAKE ME FOR?! URNf!

IT'S ALWAYS: "FONE BONE, YOU GOTTA SAVE ME!" OR: "FONE BONE, YOU GOTTA HELP ME!"

WHY, I OUGHTA--

HEY! HOW'D I GET SO CLOSE TO THE MOUNTAINS?!

WHERE IS EVERYBODY? WHERE'S TH' LOCUSTS?!

NO WAY! I CLIMBED UP THE WRONG SIDE! PHONEY! HELP!! YOU GOTTA SAVE ME!!

HUH
HUH
HUH

HUFF!

WHERE TH' HECK **ARE** THOSE GUYS? WE'RE GOIN' STRAIGHT INTO TH' MOUNTAINS!

I HOPE I CATCH UP TO 'EM BEFORE IT GETS DARK . . . .

THE **LAST** THING I WANT TO DO IS SPEND THE NIGHT OUT HERE BY MYSELF!

. . . OF COURSE, AFTER A DAY LIKE **TODAY**, IT'S HARD TO IMAGINE THAT ANYTHING **WORSE** COULD HAPPEN . . .

YAWN!

OH, **MAN!** THIS AIN'T GONNA **CUT IT!**

I ACTUALLY THOUGHT THIS MAP WOULD TAKE ME THROUGH TH' MOUNTAINS TO THIS WATERFALL ON HERE . . .

. . . BUT IF THIS THING WERE **REAL**, I WOULD'VE COME TO TH' PASS BY **NOW!** ERRR! I'M SO **STUPID!** I BET THIS MAP WAS JUST ONE OF SMILEY'S **PRANKS** — — AND I **FELL** FOR IT!

AND TO TOP IT **OFF**, I HAVEN'T SEEN ANY MORE **CIGAR BUTTS** ALL DAY . . . **HOW** DO I GET MYSELF **INTO** THESE THINGS?

OH, WELL . . . I'LL FIND THOSE GUYS **SOONER** OR LATER . . . **IF** I DON'T DIE OF THIRST . . .

UNTIL **THEN**, I JUST GOTTA KEEP MOVIN'! KEEP . . .

COOL.

I MADE IT!

THAT STUPID MAP WAS **RIGHT!** YESSIREE, **BOB!** THERE'S WATER ON TH' MENU **TONIGHT!**

I COULD **KISS** SMILEY BONE FOR FINDING THAT MAP!

I MIGHT EVEN KISS **PHONEY** RIGHT BEFORE I STRANGLE HIM!

AND LOOK! ONE OF SMILEY'S **CIGAR STUBS!**

HEY! WATCH IT! YOU ALMOST STEPPED ON ME!

WHOOPS! HELLO! WHAT ARE **YOU** SUPPOSED TO BE?

I'M TED! I'M A BUG!

YOU LOOK MORE LIKE A **LEAF!**

A **LEAF?!** THAT'S A **INSULT!** WHERE'S MY BIG BROTHER?

HEY, HOLD ON! I DIDN'T MEAN ANY HARM! BESIDES, WHAT COULD **YOUR** BIG BROTHER DO TO ME?

WHOA.

IS YOU PICKIN' ON TED?

I - - JUST SAID HE LOOKS LIKE A LEAF!

WHAT ARE YOU? A TROUBLE-MAKER? WE DON'T NEED YOUR KIND IN OUR VALLEY!

I GUESS HE DIDN'T MEAN NO HARM, BIG BROTHER! YOU DON'T HAS TO HIT HIM IF YOU DON'T WANT!

LISTEN TO HIM! LISTEN TO HIM!

WELL, OKAY, TED, IF YOU SAY SO . . . .

I'M NOT TRYIN' TO CAUSE TROUBLE! I'M LOOKING FOR MY COUSINS! WE GOT SEPARATED, AN' NOW I'M LOST! YOU WOULDN'T KNOW HOW TO GET TO **BONEVILLE** FROM HERE, WOULD YA?

BONEVILLE? NEVER HEARD OF IT . . .

BUT YOU BETTER FIND IT -- **FAST!** IT'S AUTUMN NOW, AN' WINTER STRIKES **QUICK** IN THESE PARTS . . . AN' WHEN IT DOES, **NOBODY** CAN GET THROUGH THOSE MOUNTAINS . . .

. . . IN **OR** OUT!

SO I SUGGEST YOU MAKE YOUR VISIT HERE A **SHORT** ONE, OR YOU'LL BE STUCK FOR TH' WINTER. AN' I DON'T THINK YOU WANNA **DO** THAT!

NO. DEFINITELY NOT.

GOOD. I'LL LET YA GO FOR **NOW**, SINCE TED SEEMS TO LIKE YA OKAY . . . BUT DON'T FERGET!

NO DAWDLIN'!

THANK YOU FOR NOT HITTING ME.

DON'T WORRY 'BOUT HIM . . . HE'S ACTUAL A REAL NICE GUY!

WELL . . . NOW WE GOTTA FIGGER OUT WHAT TA **DO** WITH YA . . . SAY! I KNOW! I'LL TAKE YA TO SEE THORN! C'MON! WHAT'S YER **NAME**, MISTER?

FONE BONE. SO WHO'S THIS THORN? HE'S NOT ANOTHER **BIG BUG**, IS HE?

HO, HO! NO! THORN KNOWS JES' ABOUT EVER'THIN' IN TH' **WHOLE WORLD!**

BUT, LISTEN, BONE! BIG BROTHER WAS RIGHT ABOUT WINTER! SHE HITS **FAST!** 'N' IF YOU WANTS TA GIT HOME, YOU GOTTA DO IT BEFORE SHE **SNOWS!**

DON'T WORRY! I'M JUST GONNA FIND MY COUSINS, AN' THEN I'M **OUTTA HERE!**

TED! WAIT FOR ME!

WELL, WELL... LOOK WHO'S JOINED US FOR SUPPER... GO START THE COOKING FIRE!!

NO, YOU CALLED ME FAT.

NO?!! WHAT DO YOU MEAN NO?!!

AND IT'S NOT THE FIRST TIME YOU'VE DONE IT, EITHER...

COMRADE... BE REASONABLE! I WASN'T THINKING--- I WAS TRYING TO CATCH OUR DINNER--- THIS ISN'T THE TIME---

I TAKE IT BACK.... YOU'RE NOT FAT.

TOO LATE!

PLEASE, COMRADE! I JUST WANT TO CHOP HIM UP FOR THE STEW!

AND THAT'S ANOTHER THING! I'M TIRED OF STEW! I WANT TO PUT HIM IN A CRUST AND BAKE A LIGHT FLUFFY QUICHE!

QUICHE?! WHAT KIND OF FOOD IS THAT FOR A MONSTER TO EAT?!..... LISTEN, DO YOU THINK YOU COULD COME BACK IN HALF AN HOUR? WE'LL HAVE THIS STRAIGHTENED OUT BY THEN!

WHY DIDN'T YOU STOP ME?

WHY SHOULD I? YOU'RE SO SMART!

TED!

C'MON, TED! WHERE **ARE** YOU? YOU GOTTA TAKE ME TO SEE THORN.'

-- I'M SORRY I CALLED YOU A **LEAF**!

WHOOOOOP! WATER! I HEAR **WATER**!!

WATER!

WATER! WATER!

WATER! MMMM **WATER**! WATER! MMMM WATER! WATER! MMMMMM MM MM OH, **MAN**!

WHAT AM I GONNA **DO**? WHAT IF I **CAN'T** FIND MY COUSINS BEFORE IT **SNOWS**? WE COULD BE **TRAPPED** HERE FOR TH' WHOLE **WINTER**!

I **GOTTA** GET OUTTA HERE! THIS FOREST IS TOO **WEIRD** FOR ME!

RUMMMBLE

HELLO, MIZ 'POSSUM! I HAVEN'T SEEN **YOU** IN A COUPLE OF MONTHS!

OH, I DON'T GET OUT OF TH' HOUSE MUCH IN **WINTER** 'SPECIALLY WITH **YOUNGUNS!**

THESE CAN'T BE **YOUR** KIDS! THEY'RE ALL GROWN UP!

WELL, IT'S ALMOST **SPRING!** THEY SHOOT UP **FAST** THIS TIME OF YEAR! YOU BOYS REMEMBER FONE BONE?

SURE!

YEAH!

HOW YOU GUYS DOIN'?

WE'RE COOL!

WHERE'D YA GET TH' **HAT?**

YOUR MOM MADE IT FOR ME!

PRETTY DORKY!

MOM BROUGHT YA SOME MORE **BLANKETS 'N' STUFF!**

WOW! THANKS! I DON'T KNOW **HOW** I WOULD'VE MADE IT THROUGH TH' WINTER WITHOUT YOU, MIZ 'POSSUM!

DON'T YOU **WORRY** ABOUT IT! AS LONG AS YOU'RE STUCK HERE IN OUR VALLEY, **I'LL** TAKE CARE OF YOU! HERE! I PACKED A PIE IN CASE YOU'RE HUNGRY!

DID YOU EVER FIND THOSE COUSINS OF YOURS?

NO, NOT YET. HAVE YOU SEEN **TED** SINCE I TALKED TO YOU LAST?

NOPE. DON'T KNOW MUCH ABOUT WHAT BUGS **DO** IN TH' WINTER, BUT I HAVEN'T SEEN WING **NOR** ANTENNAE OF TED SINCE TH' **SNOW** HIT...

SAY... WASN'T THERE SOMEONE **ELSE** YOU WANTED ME TO FIND OUT ABOUT?

TED WAS GONNA TAKE ME TO SEE SOMEONE NAMED **THORN.**

OH, THAT'S RIGHT! NOPE, HAVEN'T FOUND OUT A **THING!** YOU SURE YOU HAVE ENOUGH BLANKETS?

YES, MA'M. SIGH. WELL, THANKS ANYWAY, MIZ 'POSSUM! IF THERE'S EVER ANYTHING I CAN **DO** --

AS A MATTER OF **FACT**, I'M ON MY WAY OVER TO MIZ HEDGEHOG'S PLACE, 'N' I WAS WONDERIN' IF YOU'D MIND WATCHIN' TH' KIDS?

ALL **RIGHT!** WE'RE GONNA STAY WITH FONE BONE!

ME?! BUT... **I** DON'T KNOW ANYTHING ABOUT BABY 'POSSUMS!

IT'LL JUST BE FOR AN HOUR OR TWO! YOU BOYS BE **GOOD** NOW!

DON'T WORRY ABOUT **US**, MOM!

WELL ... C'MON, GUYS. YOU CAN HELP ME PUT THE **FINISHING** TOUCH ON MY HOUSE!

RUN INSIDE WHERE IT'S WARM ... I'LL JUST BE A SECOND!

WHOOP!

YIPPEE!

THERE WE GO! COZY AS AN IGLOO! BY THE TIME THIS MELTS, IT'LL BE **SPRING**, AN' THEN I'M **OUTTA** HERE!

SMASH! CRASH!

HEY, GUYS! TAKE IT **EASY** IN TH--

CRUNCH

WHAT TH' HECK WAS THAT?

HOLY COW!

WHAT ARE YOU TRYING TO **DO**?!! **KILL** EACH OTHER? C'MON, LET'S SIT BY THE FIREPLACE, AN' I'LL TELL YOU A STORY!

AW! WE WERE HAVIN' **FUN**!

WE DON'T **WANNA** HEAR A STORY!

WE WANNA **PLAY**!

HE CAN'T PLAY WITH US! HE DON'T KNOW **NUTHIN'** 'BOUT BABY 'POSSUMS! HE **SAID** SO!

PLAY WITH US, MR. BONE!

YEAH! C'MON!

WHAT DO YOU WANNA PLAY?

WHAT 'POSSUMS PLAY **BEST** IS PLAY "DEAD"!

LOOK OUT! IT'S A GIANT 'POSSUM-EATING BEAR!!

HMM!

I KINDA **LIKE** THIS GAME.

HEH, HEH! LOOK AT 'EM! THEY LOOK LIKE LITTLE ANGELS! I GUESS BABYSITTING WON'T BE SO TOUGH **AFTER** ALL!

♪

HEE HEE HEE

HERE COMES THE **BEAR!** YOU BETTER WATCH OUT! I'M GONNA **EAT YOU UP!**

RRRRRRRRRR!

WHEEE!

HA! HA!

RUN! TH' BEAR IS **CHASIN' US!**

HEY! STAY IN TH' HOUSE!

THOSE RAT CREATURES WOULD HAVE TO BE PRETTY STUPID TO FOLLOW ME ON TO THIS FRAIL, LITTLE BRANCH.'

STUPID, STUPID RAT CREATURES!!

SNAP!

GASP!

OW!

UH ... WELL ... IT WAS NICE MEETING YOU, BUT I BETTER GO FIND TH' KIDS!

WHOA.

DON'T WORRY ABOUT THE KIDS. THEY'RE SAFE.

GO STRAIGHT DOWN THE HILL. IT'S A SHORTCUT TO MIZ 'POSSUM'S HOUSE.

... UH ... SURE! THANKS!

!

HEY! HOW'D YOU KNOW I WAS LOOKING FOR MIZ 'POSSUM'S KIDS?!

BONE!

BONE! THERE YOU ARE! WE CAME AS FAST AS WE COULD! ARE YOU ALL RIGHT?

YAY!

HE'S SAFE!

I'M OKAY... I HAD A LITTLE RUN-IN WITH A DRAGON, BUT THE IMPORTANT THING IS THAT WE'RE ALL SAFE!

A DRAGON? REALLY?

GET OUTTA TOWN!

SEE HOW HE IS WITH TH' KIDS? HE'S ALWAYS GOT A STORY!

IT'S NOT ENOUGH THAT HE CHASED OFF THOSE BULLIES... NOW HE'S TURNED IT INTO A YARN WITH A DRAGON IN IT!

ISN'T THAT PRECIOUS?

WHAT WAS THAT?

OH! I'M SORRY, BONE! TEE HEE! GO AHEAD AN' TELL TH' BOYS ABOUT TH' FEROCIOUS FIRE-BREATHING DRAGON!

YEAH! TELL US! WERE YOU SCARED?

OF COURSE I WAS!

HE'S SO MODEST!

AND BRAVE!

WHAT HAPPENED, FONE BONE? DID YOU KILL TH' DRAGON?

WHAT HAPPENED TO YOUR HAT? DID THE DRAGON DO IT?

HE'S PULLIN' OUR TAILS! EVERYBODY KNOWS DRAGONS ARE MAKE-BELIEVE!

AREN'T THEY?!

THAT'S ENOUGH QUESTIONS FOR NOW. UNCLE BONE MUST BE VERY TIRED. LET'S ALL GO HOME WHERE IT'S WARM AND SAFE, AND THEN BONE CAN TELL US ALL ABOUT HIS ADVENTURE!

MAYBE HE'D LIKE TO STOP AND CLEAN UP FIRST.

OH, YES! BY ALL **MEANS!** THERE'S A NICE, HOT **SPRING** JUST BACK OVER TH' HILL! WHY DON'T YOU STOP THERE TO FRESHEN UP! C'MON ALONG, BOYS! SAY THANK YOU TO UNCLE BONE!

THANK YOU!

DID HE REALLY SEE A DRAGON?

NOW, DEAR...

HMMF! DID **TOO** SEE A DRAGON!

WHAT DO THEY **THINK?** I LIT MY **HEAD** ON FIRE TO KEEP WARM?

...AN' HOW COME THAT DRAGON KNEW I WAS BABYSITTING TH' **'POSSUM** KIDS? WHAT'S HE DOIN'? **FOLLOWIN'** ME AROUND?

THIS PLACE IS **TOO** WEIRD! THE FIRST SIGN OF SPRING I SEE... **POW!** I'M TAKIN' OFF **RIGHT** THROUGH THOSE MOUNTAINS! WITH OR **WITHOUT** MY COUSINS!

SNAP!

UH, OH. WHAT WAS THAT?

♪ MMMMMM ♪

¡FOOM!

WHY, YES! I KNOW TED! HE'S A **VERY** GOOD FRIEND OF MINE!

HOTCHA! THIS IS **GREAT!**

I'VE BEEN LOOKIN' FOR YOU **ALL** **WINTER!!**

YOU HAVE? WHY?

TED! HE TOLD ME TO FIND YOU! HE SAID THAT YOU KNOW **EVERYTHING!**

WELL, THAT CERTAINLY **SOUNDS** LIKE TED.

GREAT! THEN YOU CAN HELP ME AND MY COUSINS GET BACK TO **BONEVILLE?**

COUSINS? YOU MEAN THERE'S **MORE** OF YOU?

YEAH! THEY'RE STUCK IN THIS VALLEY, TOO! BUT I HAVEN'T SEEN EITHER ONE OF 'EM SINCE WE GOT HIT BY THAT SWARM OF **LOCUSTS!**

YOU DON'T SAY.

Y'KNOW. . . I **SHOULD'VE** ASKED THAT **DRAGON** IF HE'D SEEN MY COUSINS!

YOU SHOULD'VE ASKED **WHO?**

THE **DRAGON!** OH ... WAIT A MINUTE! **I** GET IT! YOU DON'T BELIEVE IN DRAGONS, **DO** YOU?

NO. SHOULD **I?**

NEVER MIND! I DON'T **CARE!**

ONCE I'M BACK IN **BONEVILLE,** I'LL NEVER EVEN HAVE TO **THINK** ABOUT DRAGONS OR THIS CRAZY VALLEY **AGAIN!**

WELL, I'D **LIKE** TO HELP...

WELL, C'MON! THERE'S NO TIME TO LOSE!!

...BUT... I'VE NEVER **HEARD** OF BONEVILLE. THERE **IS** A LITTLE VILLAGE DOWN THE ROAD CALLED BARRELHAVEN ... DOES THAT HELP?

...WHAT'S WRONG?

NOTHIN'

FONE BONE?

OH . . . I DON'T BELONG IN THIS FOREST. MY HOME'S ON THE OTHER SIDE OF THE MOUNTAINS . . .

I'M SURE WE CAN GET YOU THROUGH THE MOUNTAINS AS SOON AS THE SNOW MELTS!

IT'S NOT JUST THAT! EVEN IF I **COULD** GET THROUGH THE MOUNTAINS, I'D **NEVER** FIND MY WAY BACK ACROSS THE DESERT. YOU WERE MY LAST HOPE.

WELL, LET'S JUST CONCENTRATE ON FINDING YOUR COUSINS. YOU'RE **SURE** THEY'RE HERE IN THE VALLEY?

PRETTY SURE, UNLESS THE RAT CREATURES GOT 'EM.

DID YOU SAY **RAT CREATURES**?

LET ME GUESS . . . YOU DON'T **BELIEVE** IN RAT CREATURES.

OH, YES I **DO!** HAVE YOU SEEN ONE **RECENTLY**?

I SAW **TWO** OF 'EM! TH' DRAGON CHASED 'EM OFF!

NOW LISTEN TO ME . . . THIS IS IMPORTANT! YOU'RE NOT FOOLING AROUND? YOU **REALLY** SAW TWO RAT CREATURES?

YEAH! I REALLY SAW A **DRAGON**, TOO! LOOK AT MY **HEAD!** WHAT DO YOU THINK **THIS** IS? A **TAN?!**

MY! YOU MUST'VE **ENJOYED** YOUR FIRST NIGHT IN A HOUSE AFTER SLEEPING IN THE **WOODS**! YOU DIDN'T EVEN **HEAR** ME WHEN I CAME DOWNSTAIRS!

CAKES?

HERE'S YOUR CAKES! AND HERE'S SOME TEA!

THENK YOU.

HELLO? ARE YOU **AWAKE** YET, FONE BONE? IT'S **ME**, THORN!

THORN?

AH! YOU'RE AWAKE! GOOD! NOW EAT YOUR BREAKFAST! WE'VE GOT A LOT TO **DO** TODAY! GRAN'MA BEN IS COMING HOME FROM THE VILLAGE, AND I WANT TO CLEAN THE PLACE UP BEFORE SHE GETS HERE!

SHE'S COMING HOME **TODAY**?

THAT'S **RIGHT**! SHE GOES INTO **BARRELHAVEN** EVERY SPRING TO SHOW OFF HER BEST **RACING COWS**!

YOUR GRAN'MA RACES **COWS**?!

YEAH! SHE'S PRETTY **GOOD**, TOO! THERE'S HARDLY A COW IN THE WHOLE **VALLEY** THAT CAN BEAT HER IN A **100-YARD DASH**!

HUH! I'M **DEFINITELY** LOOKING FORWARD TO **MEETING** THIS LADY!

OH, IT'S A **BIG EVENT** HERE IN THE SPRING! PEOPLE BET **CHICKENS** AND **GOATS** -- SOME FOLKS BET THEIR WHOLE LIVESTOCK ON HER! IF YOU WANT TO MAKE A GOOD IMPRESSION, BE SURE TO COMPLIMENT HER ON HER **COWS**! SHE'S **REAL** PROUD OF HER COWS!

I'LL TRY TO REMEMBER THAT.

NOW, IF YOU'RE DONE EATING, WHY DON'T WE GO GET SOME WATER?

OKAY BY ME! LET'S **DO IT**!

HOW ABOUT IF WE GET THE FIREWOOD **LATER?**

SIGH.

SO ... DO YOU THINK YOUR GRAN'MA WILL MIND ME **STAYIN'** WITH YOU GUYS? I MEAN-- I DON'T WANNA CAUSE ANY PROBLEMS!

SHE WON'T MIND! SHE WOULDN'T MAKE YOU GO BACK OUT IN THE **WOODS** -- ESPECIALLY WITH THOSE **RAT CREATURES** AROUND!

I HOPE NOT.

JUST DO ME ONE FAVOR! WHEN GRAN'MA BEN GETS HERE, **TRY** NOT TO MENTION YOUR FRIEND THE **DRAGON!**

WHY NOT?

BECAUSE DRAGONS DON'T **EXIST**, THAT'S WHY!

WHAT DO YOU **MEAN?** YOU BELIEVE IN **RAT CREATURES!** WHY DON'T YOU BELIEVE IN **DRAGONS?**

BECAUSE **EVERYBODY** BELIEVES IN RAT CREATURES! BUT **YOU'RE** THE ONLY ONE WHO'S EVER SEEN A **DRAGON!**

I DON'T BELIEVE IT!

DO YOU HAVE DRAGONS BACK IN **BONEVILLE**?

OF COURSE **NOT**!

WELL?

WELL, WE DON'T HAVE BIGMOUTHED, DROOLING, **RAT-LIKE** MONSTERS, EITHER! UNLESS YOU COUNT MY COUSIN **PHONEY BONE**!

AN' YOU KNOW WHAT **ELSE**? I THINK THAT DRAGON IS FOLLOWIN' ME **AROUND**!

FONE BONE! WE'VE BEEN OVER THIS A HUNDRED TIMES!

BUT I'M TELLIN' YA, I **SAW** ONE! HE HAD A GOATEE, 'N' A CIGARETTE, 'N' BIG OL' HAIRY EARS LIKE **THIS**!

DRAGONS ARE MAKE-BELIEVE! YOU WERE SEEING THINGS!

THANKS FOR THE SUPPORT, THORN! YOU KNOW, THAT'S WHAT THE DRAGON **WANTS** YOU TO THINK! HE DOESN'T WANT YOU TO KNOW HE **EXISTS**!

ACTUALLY, I JUST WANT HER TO THINK YOU'RE **NUTS**!

OH, SHUT **UP**!

YOU **HAVEN'T**? YOU MUST'VE HAD A DEPRIVED CHILDHOOD. **THESE** I BROUGHT FOR PHONEY BONE ... THEY'RE **FINANCIAL MAGAZINES!**

DIDN'T YOU BRING ANYTHING FOR YOURSELF?

SURE! THIS IS **MOBY DICK!** IT'S MY **FAVORITE BOOK!** I'VE READ IT **THREE TIMES!**

WHAT'S IT ABOUT?

UH ... ARE YOU **SURE** YOU WANT TO KNOW? EVERY TIME I TRY TO TELL PEOPLE ABOUT MOBY DICK THEIR **EYES** GLAZE OVER!

TRY ME.

OKAY! IT'S ABOUT A WHALING VOYAGE, AN' THIS GUY **ISHMAEL**

Z

HA. HA. **VERY** FUNNY.

WHAT ELSE HAVE YOU GOT IN HERE?

LET'S SEE ... A BLANKET ... AN OLD MAP THAT SMILEY FOUND ......

THAT'S ABOUT **IT!** THE ONE THING I DIDN'T BRING ENOUGH OF WAS **FOOD** AND **WATER!** WELL, TH' **TWO** THINGS ....

WHY ARE YOU MAKING THAT FACE?

I DON'T KNOW .... SOMETHING ABOUT THIS MAP IS FAMILIAR ...

REALLY? SMILEY FOUND IT OUT IN TH' DESERT RIGHT BEFORE WE GOT SPLIT UP.

IT REMINDS ME OF A DREAM I USED TO HAVE ...

WHOA. AND YOU THINK **MY** STORIES ARE STRANGE!

ARE YOU OKAY?

I'M FINE, LET'S JUST FORGET IT. C'MON, GRAN'MA WILL BE HERE SOON ...

SLURK
GUKK
BURRRRP!

SIGH.

WHAT A **TRAVESTY!** TH' MOST **CHERISHED** AND **RESPECTED** (NOT TO MENTION WEALTHIEST!) BONE IN BONEVILLE-- OUT IN TH' WOODS-- FENDING OFF TH' ELEMENTS WITH HIS BARE HANDS!

FORCED TO EKE OUT A MISERABLE EXISTENCE **AMIDST TH' ROCKS'N'MUD!!**

OH, CRUEL, CRUEL, FATE! WHY HAVE YOU ABANDONED YOUR MOST BELOVED SON?!

GOD, I PITY ME.

HEY, YOU! WAKE UP!

MM?

THE NAME'S PHONEY BONE ... TH' **RICHEST** BONE IN BONEVILLE! YOU'VE PROBABLY **HEARD** OF ME! I'M LOOKIN' FOR A GUY NAMED FONE BONE. YOU SEEN HIM?

HEY! LET'S KICK THAT PEA-SIZED **DINOSAUR BRAIN** INTO HIGH GEAR, HUH?

WOULD IT HELP IF I ASKED TH' QUESTION AGAIN **SLOWER?**

HAVE......**YOU**.....

...SEEN FONE BONE..... ..... A-**ROUND?**

UH, HEY, THERE, MISTER! MAYBE YOU BETTER LET **ME** HELP YOU!

MAYBE I **BETTER!** IT COULD BE **DAYS** BEFORE TH' MESSAGE REACHES **THIS** GUY'S BRAIN!

HOW 'BOUT WE TAKE A FEW STEPS OFF TO STARBOARD... OUTTA **FIRIN' RANGE**... AN' **I'LL** ANSWER YER QUESTIONS FOR YA.

OH, YEAH? AN' WHO ARE YOU?

I'M TED! I'M A BUG!

SPARE ME TH' **DETAILS**, FRIEND! I'M LOOKIN' FOR A GUY NAMED FONE BONE. YOU **SEEN** HIM?

BONE?! OH, YEAH! I SEEN HIM!

YOU **HAVE?!** I'M **SAVED!** WHERE IS HE?

DON'T KNOW. AIN'T SEEN HIM SINCE BEFORE SHE **SNOWED.**

HA! A **LIKELY** STORY! BUG! TAKE ME TO YOUR **LEADER!**

TAKE YOU TO MY LEADER?

C'MON! C'MON! I AIN'T GOT ALL DAY!

WHO SHOULD I TAKES YA TO?

I NEED **ANSWERS**, BUG! I DEMAND **SATISFACTION!**

I GUESS I COULD TAKE YA TO SEE THORN'S GRAN'MA...

FINE. FINE. WHAT- EVER!

BUT I GOTS TA WARN YA... SHE'S A **OL'** LADY, AN' SHE MIGHT NOT TAKE TO YER ATTITUDE MUCH...

DON'T WORRY ABOUT **ME**, BUG! THERE AIN'T A WOMAN **ALIVE** WHO CAN RESIST MY CHARMS!

OKEE DOKEE... I WAS JES' WARNIN' YA, THAT'S ALL.

WELL, MOVE IT OUT, BUG! THIS IS TAKING FOREVER ON THOSE LITTLE LEGS OF YOURS!

OKEE DOKEE...

HI, GRAN'MA! HOW YOU DOIN'?

WELL, HELLO, TED, DEAR!

GRAN'MA, THIS HERE FELLA BEEN ASKIN' TA MEET YA!

OH, HE LOOKS LIKE SUCH A NICE YOUNG MAN. WOULD HE LIKE TO RIDE ONE OF MY RACING COWS?

NO, I DON'T WANNA RIDE ONE OF YER STUPID COWS!

TED, DEAR, I THINK YOU'D BETTER LEAVE. I'M GONNA TEAR THIS LITTLE FELLA APART FROM THE INSIDE OUT.

YES, MA'M. (SEE YA AROUND, PAL.)

DO YOU LIKE APPLE PIE, FONE BONE?

LIKE IT? IT'S MY FAVORITE HOBBY!

WELL, DON'T GET **TOO** EXCITED!

THIS IS FOR GRAN'MA -- SHE **LOVES** MY SPECIAL APPLE PIE...

...AND WE WANT TO BE **REAL** NICE TO GRAN'MA BEFORE WE ASK ABOUT YOU **STAYING HERE!**

CLINK CLINK

HEY! WHAT'S GOIN' ON?! TH' WHOLE CABIN'S STARTIN' TO SHAKE!

IT'S GRAN'MA! SHE'S HOME!

YOUR GRAN'MA?! IT SOUNDS LIKE A STAMPEDE!

THAT'S HER! SHE MUST BE RACING ONE OF THE COWS!

LOOK OUTSIDE! THAT'S HER FASTEST COW COMING ACROSS THE CLEARING!

NO WAY!

AND HERE COMES GRAN'MA! C'MON, GRAN'MA!

SHE'S GONNA OUTRUN THAT COW?! SHE'LL HAVE A HEART ATTACK!

HEY! DO YOU SEE THAT? THERE'S SOMETHING ON THE COW.

WHAT? WHERE?

--THERE'S SOMEONE RIDING THE COW!

OH, MY GOD! IT'S PHONEY BONE!

WHAT HAPPENED TO **PHONEY**?

-- UH, OH --

I **THINK** HE'S IN THE **FIREPLACE**!

I'M COMIN', PHONEY!

HURRY, GRAN'MA! HE'S **STUCK** IN THE **FIREPLACE!**

OH, MY GOODNESS! HE'LL RUIN TH' DINNER!

HANG ON! I'LL GET YOU OUT!

FONE BONE! SAVE ME! THAT CRAZY OLD LADY TRIED TO **KILL ME!!**

WELL, BLESS MY **BUTTONS!** WHAT HAVE WE GOT HERE?

WATCH OUT! DON'T LET HER GET AHOLD OF YOU!

H-- H'LO, MA'M!

DO **YOU** LIKE COWS? I KNOW YOUR **FRIEND** DOESN'T.

I DON'T LIKE TO **RIDE 'EM,** YOU OL' BAT!

FONE BONE LOVES COWS!

SORRY, DEAR. YOU CAN'T KEEP HIM.

GRAN'MA, THEY'RE **BONES**! THEY COME FROM A PLACE CALLED BONEVILLE! AND THEY NEED OUR HELP TO GET **BACK**!

WHERE'S SMILEY?

SMILEY? I THOUGHT HE WAS WITH **YOU**!

YOU HAVEN'T SEEN HIM SINCE WE SPLIT UP? BUT I **KNOW** HE'S IN TH' VALLEY! I FOUND ONE OF HIS **CIGAR BUTTS**!

TH' LAST TIME I SAW THAT CHOWDERHEAD, HE WAS SAYIN' HOW **COOL** IT WAS THAT WE WERE ABOUT TO BE PULVERIZED BY INSECTS!

YEAH! THAT'S TH' LAST TIME I SAW HIM, TOO. . .

AW, QUIT YER **WORRYIN'**! WHY DON'T YA INTRODUCE ME TO YER GOOD-LOOKIN' **FRIEND**, HERE?

OH! UH. . . PHONEY, THIS IS THORN! THORN, PHONEY.

SO, WHAT'VE YOU BEEN DOIN' WITH MY COUSIN? YOU TWO GOT A LITTLE **THING** GOIN', OR WHAT?

PHONEY!

NO, HUH? FIGURES! WHAT'D YA **DO**? **BORE** HER TO DEATH TALKIN' ABOUT **MOBY DICK**?

I'M GOING TO BED. YOU CAN KEEP 'EM IF YOU WANT, BUT THEY HAVE TO SLEEP IN TH' BARN.

GRAM!

G'NIGHT MA'M IT WAS NICE MEETING YOU!

FONE BONE, COULD I TALK TO YOU FOR A MOMENT? OUTSIDE?

YES.

WELL, GO AHEAD! I AIN'T STOPPIN' YA!

THIS ISN'T GOING QUITE THE WAY WE **PLANNED**, IS IT? TELL ME... IS HE **ALWAYS** LIKE THIS?

PRETTY MUCH.

HMM. GRAN'MA'S GOING BACK TO **BARRELHAVEN** IN A FEW DAYS FOR THE SPRING FESTIVAL. IF WE CAN JUST KEEP THOSE TWO **CALM** UNTIL **THEN**, WE CAN ALL GO INTO TOWN TOGETHER TO LOOK FOR YOUR OTHER COUSIN.

DON'T WORRY! I CAN HANDLE PHONEY!

GO BACK IN THE HOUSE AND KEEP AN **EYE** ON HIM. I HAVE TO GO GET SOME FRESH WATER FOR GRAN'MA TO WASH UP WITH ...

OKAY, PHONEY! WE HAVE TO GET A COUPLE OF THINGS STRAIGHT---

WHAT ARE YOU **DOING** ?!! THAT PIE WAS FOR GRAN'MA BEN! THORN WILL **KILL** US WHEN SHE FINDS OUT YOU TOOK IT!

WHAT'S TH' MATTER? YOU AFRAID OF GETTIN' **CAUGHT**? QUIT BEIN' A **CHICKEN!**

FONE BONE!! PHONEY BONE!! YOU BETTER NOT BE EATING THAT **PIE!**

HONK!

WELL, BOYS . . . I CAN SEE **WE'RE** OFF TO A GOOD START!

WE HAVEN'T SEEN IT! HONEST!

ERP!

COME ON! A LITTLE HONEST WORK ISN'T GOING TO KILL YOU!

A **LITTLE**?! THAT CRAZY OL' LADY IS RUNNIN' OUR **BUTTS** OFF! MILK TH' COWS! **FEED** TH' COWS! TAKE CARE OF TH' **CHICKENS**!

GRAN'MA BEN IS **FEEDING** US **AND** LETTIN' US STAY IN HER BARN! TH' **LEAST** WE CAN DO IS HELP OUT!

TH' BARN **STINKS**, AND IT'S **DRAFTY**! IF IT WASN'T FOR TH' **FOOD**, I'D RATHER TAKE MY CHANCES BACK OUT IN TH' **WOODS**!

WE'RE GONNA **END UP** IN TH' WOODS IF YOU DON'T CLEAN THIS UP AN' GET ANOTHER BUCKET OF **MILK**!

I SHOULD'VE **KNOWN** YOU WOULDN'T UNDERSTAND! YOU NEVER HAD ANY **REAL** MONEY! YOU DON'T KNOW WHAT IT'S **LIKE** TO LOSE EVERYTHING! **YOU** DON'T KNOW WHAT IT'S LIKE TO BE **BROKE**!

I'M **HERE**, AREN'T I? BESIDES, YOU'RE **NOT BROKE**! YOU'VE STILL GOT A WAD OF BILLS ON YOU!

ONLY A COUPLE OF THOUSAND... STILL, THEY **DO** GIVE ME **SOME** COMFORT! LOOK! AREN'T THEY BEAUTIFUL?

AAAAH!

THEY'RE GETTING **WRINKLED**! I'M TELLIN' YA, FONE BONE, I CAN'T **TAKE** MUCH MORE OF THIS!!

IT'S NOT FOR MUCH **LONGER**! AS SOON AS WE FIND SMILEY BONE WE'RE GONNA GET OUTTA HERE! UNTIL **THEN**, JUST **TRY** NOT TO GET US KICKED OFF TH' FARM, OKAY?

ALL RIGHT, ALL RIGHT. COOL YER JETS! I'LL TRY NOT TO CAUSE ANY TROUBLE.

GOOD! I'VE GOTTA GO FIND **THORN** ... I PROMISED I'D HELP HER CHURN BUTTER TODAY!

YEAH, YEAH. STICK SOME HAY IN MY TEETH AN' CALL ME GOOBER!

CHEER UP, PHONEY! **BREAKFAST** WILL BE READY SOON!

RRRRR.

MORNIN', BONE!

GOOD MORNIN', GRAN'MA! YOU ALL SET FOR OUR BIG TRIP TO **BARRELHAVEN** TOMORROW?

I'M STILL **PACKIN'**-- I SEEM TO BE MISSING A PAIR OF **BLOOMERS**, THOUGH ... YOU AN' YOUR COUSIN WOULDN'T KNOW ANYTHING ABOUT THAT, WOULD YOU?

NO, MA'M!

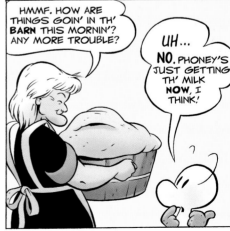

HMMF. HOW ARE THINGS GOIN' IN TH' **BARN** THIS MORNIN'? ANY MORE TROUBLE?

UH... **NO.** PHONEY'S JUST GETTING TH' MILK **NOW**, I THINK!

THAT'S GOOD. WE'VE GOT A TIGHT SCHEDULE ----

YES, MA'M! THORN AND I ARE GOING TO CHURN BUTTER, AND BAKE THESE LITTLE BREAD THINGS WITH STUFF IN 'EM TO TAKE ON TH' JOURNEY-

OH, NO . . . .

WHAT?

DON'T YOU WANT TH' BREAD THINGS?

IT'S NOT TH' **BREAD**, BONE! IT'S TH' **GITCHY FEELIN'**! --IT JUST COME **AT** ME OUTTA TH' **BLUE**!

TH' GITCHY FEELIN'? WHAT'S THAT?

TH' **GITCHY**! IT'S A **TERRIBLE** FEELIN' THAT MAKES YOUR HEAD **SWIM**, AN' YOUR LEGS **WOBBLE**! IT'S A POWERFUL **OMEN** OF **BAD THINGS** TO **COME**!

. . .THERE . . . IT'S STARTIN' TO PASS. MAYBE WHATEVER'S GOIN' TO HAPPEN WON'T BE SO BAD. . .

ARE YOU OKAY?

IT'S GONE NOW. BUT TH' GITCHY FEELIN' IS **NEVER** WRONG! YOU KEEP AN EYE ON THAT COUSIN OF YOURS, YOU HEAR?

YES MA'M!

PHONEY! DID YOU DO SOMETHING WITH GRAN'MA BEN'S **BLOOMERS**?

YEH, I TOOK 'EM OFF TH' CLOTHES-LINE AND NAILED 'EM UP ON TH' SIDE OF TH' BARN.

YOU DID WHAT?!!

I KINDA MADE A LITTLE HOLE IN TH' WALL, AND THOSE WERE THE BIGGEST THINGS I COULD FIND TO COVER IT UP!

YOU'RE REALLY **PUSHIN'** IT, **THIS** TIME, PHONEY!

YOU CAN'T TALK THAT WAY TO ME! I'M YOUR **COUSIN**! I'M TH' **RICHEST BONE** IN **BONEVILLE**!

YOU **WERE** TH' RICHEST BONE IN BONEVILLE! AN' IT WAS YOUR **MONEY-GRUBBIN' SCHEMES** THAT GOT US **INTO** THIS MESS, REMEMBER?

DO YOU **HAVE** TO KEEP BRINGING THAT UP?! SO I GOT US RUN OUT OF BONEVILLE, AND A **LYNCH MOB** CHASED US FOR TWO WEEKS! **JEEZ!** ONE LITTLE MISTAKE, AND I GOTTA HEAR ABOUT IT TH' REST OF MY **LIFE**?!

MAYBE YOU'LL THINK **TWICE** NEXT TIME BEFORE YOU BUILD AN **ORPHANAGE** ON A **HAZARDOUS WASTE LANDFILL!!**

WHAT IS **WRONG** WITH **THAT**?! THAT'S **TWO** COMMUNITY SERVICES **ROLLED INTO ONE!!** IT WAS TH' **ULTIMATE TAX SHELTER!**

YOU **NEVER** LEARN, DO YOU?

I **SHOULDA** STUCK WITH MY FIRST IDEA!

WHAT? COMBINING A **SLAUGHTERHOUSE** WITH A **PETTING ZOO?!** OH, YEAH! **THAT** WAS **BRILLIANT!**

AHH! WHAT DO **YOU** KNOW?

CAN'T YOU MAKE IT THROUGH **ONE MORE DAY** WITHOUT GETTING US IN **TROUBLE?** WE'RE GOIN' INTO TOWN WITH GRAN'MA **TOMORROW!**

WHAT ARE WE WAITIN' FOR **HER** FOR? LET'S BLOW THIS POPSICLE STAND **NOW!**

TOMORROW IS TH' FIRST DAY OF TH' **SPRING FAIR!** THIS'LL BE OUR **BEST SHOT** AT FINDING SMILEY BONE!

GRAN'MA SAID THAT **LAST** WEEK PEOPLE WERE ALREADY COMIN' IN FROM **ALL OVER** TH' VALLEY- - - SETTIN' UP **BOOTHS** AN' GETTIN' **READY!**

WELL, **I** FIGURE -- IF SMILEY'S SOMEWHERE IN TH' VALLEY, HE'S **BOUND** TO HAVE HEARD ABOUT GRAN'MA'S **COW RACE!** YOU **KNOW** HOW MUCH HE LIKES TO BET ON **RACES!**

HO -- BACK UP! YOU MEAN PEOPLE ACTUALLY BET **MONEY** ON THAT OL' BAG TO BEAT A **COW** IN A **FOOTRACE?**

I **KNOW!** IT'S **CRAZY,** BUT THORN SAYS IT'S A BIG **DEAL** HERE! SOME FOLKS BET EVERYTHING THEY'VE **GOT!**

OKAY, FONE BONE! **I'LL** BE GOOD! I POSITIVELY **GUARANTEE** YOU WON'T HEAR ANOTHER **PEEP** OUTTA ME ALL DAY!

REALLY?

YEAH, NOW GET OFF MY BACK! GO CHURN SOME BUTTER WITH THORN! I'VE GOT STUFF TO DO!

WHAT? WHAT ARE YOU UP TO?

NOTHING! I SAID I WON'T MESS UP YOUR PLAN TO GO INTO TOWN TO LOOK FOR SMILEY, AN' I **MEANT** IT!

AND I WON'T HEAR A **PEEP** OUTTA YOU TH' REST OF TH' **DAY**, RIGHT?

RIGHT! JEEZ! DO YA WANT IT IN **WRITING?!**

DO YOU HAVE A PIECE OF PAPER?

I THINK I HEAR THORN CALLIN' YA.

REALLY?! OKAY, PHONEY! SEE YA TONIGHT!

YEP, YOU WON'T HEAR A **PEEP** OUTTA **ME**, 'CAUSE **I** AIN'T GONNA **BE** HERE!'

FONE BONE WON'T MIND IF I BORROW A FEW OF HIS THINGS . . . I MIGHT NEED 'EM ON MY WAY TO TOWN . . .

SOUNDS LIKE A LOTTA **MONEY'S** GONNA CHANGE HANDS TOMORROW, AN' I DON'T SEE WHY GRAN'MA BEN SHOULD **HOG** IT ALL!'

NO, SIRREE! IF THERE'S **BOOKMAKIN'** TO BE DONE, **I'M** TH' MAN TO **DO** IT!'

HEY, THORN! WHERE WE GOIN'?

DOWN TO THE SPRINGS!

OH, FONE BONE, YOU'RE GOING TO **LOVE** THE FESTIVAL! WE'LL SEE JUGGLERS, AND TUMBLERS, AND SINGERS! AND MY **FAVORITE** PART-- THE **BOOTHS!**

THERE ARE **ROWS** AND **ROWS** OF **BOOTHS**, AND YOU CAN BUY THE MOST **AMAZING** THINGS! THEY HAVE **HONEY**, AND **PEACOCK FEATHERS**, AND **SILK ROBES!**

I USUALLY ONLY GET TO LOOK-- BUT **THIS** YEAR I'M GOING TO GET A BOTTLE OF **DYE** FROM THE SOUTH, AND I'M GOING TO MAKE A BEAUTIFUL **BLUE DRESS!**

HOW COME WE DIDN'T BRING ANY BUCKETS TO CARRY TH' WATER BACK IN?

WE'RE NOT GETTING WATER.

WE'RE TAKING A BATH!

A BATH? WHAT **KIND** OF BATH?

OHMYGOSH

YOU WANT TO GET CLEANED UP FOR THE FESTIVAL, DON'T YOU? C'MON!

RRRR . THERE WAS A **PATH** HERE A **SECOND** AGO.' WHAT HAPPENED TO IT?

CRUNCH

CRACK

SNAP

WHY DOESN'T SOMEBODY BUILD SOME **ROADS** IN THIS PLACE?!

HMM. MAYBE I SHOULD LOOK INTO THAT. . . .

I COULD BUILD A **TOLL ROAD.'**

YEAH! I CAN ALMOST **HEAR** THOSE LITTLE COINS CALLING OUT TO ME **NOW--**

HELLO, BONE!

OVER HERE! IN TH' TREE!

WHAT ARE YOU KIDS DOIN' HANGIN' AROUND HERE? GET A JOB!

SORRY, MISTER! WE THOUGHT YOU WERE SOMEONE ELSE!

WE THOUGHT YOU WERE FONE BONE!

I'M HIS COUSIN.

HIS **COUSIN**? ALL **RIGHT!** YOU WANNA PLAY WITH US?

WE'RE LEARNIN' HOW TO HANG BY OUR TAILS!

NO, THANKS. I'M ON MY WAY INTO TOWN.

HEY, MISTER! YOU KNOW TH' **WAY** INTO TOWN?

YEAH. WHY?

IT'S **THAT** WAY.

OH! RIGHT!

THANKS, KID! WHEN I COME BACK, I'LL BRING YOU A **CARROT!**

A CARROT? WHAT'S HE THINK WE ARE? RABBITS?

WHAT A DORK.

LUCKY THING I RAN INTO THOSE KIDS! AS SOON AS I'M BACK ON TH' RIGHT PATH, I SHOULD GET TO BARRELHAVEN IN **NO TIME!**

TH' FIRST THING I GOTTA DO IS HIT TH' LOCAL TAVERN, AN' FIND OUT WHO'S IN TOWN TO BET ON TH' RACE...

SNIFF

SNIFF! SNIFF! OOOH! MAN! SOMETHING AROUND HERE SURE **STINKS!**

JEEZ!

IT'S GETTIN' **WORSE!**

WHOA.

WHAT TH' **HECK** ARE **THOSE** THINGS?

UH, OH! SOMEBODY'S COMIN'!

GET UP, YOU TWO.

ZZRT SNORT!

WHA--?

EVERYTHING'S READY FOR TOMORROW. I JUST WISH I COULD SHAKE THIS **GITCHY** FEELIN' I GOT!

DID YOU FIND TH' LITTLE SQUIRT?

NO. AN' MY **BOOTS** AN' **KNAPSACK** ARE MISSING, TOO! I THINK HE WENT INTO TOWN WITHOUT US!

WE LOOKED FOR HIM, BUT THERE'S NO SIGN OF HIM ON THE ROAD. WE WENT ALL THE WAY TO OLD MAN'S CAVE BEFORE IT GOT TOO DARK. I'M SURE WE'LL FIND HIM AT THE FAIR TOMORROW.

HMM. I DON'T LIKE IT. AN' THERE'S A BAD MOON OUT TONIGHT, TOO.

RUN BACK TO TH' BARN, AN' GET YOUR BLANKET. I THINK YOU BETTER COME IN TH' HOUSE WITH US TONIGHT.

OKAY.

OUT FROM BONEVILLE

....APPROACH ME....

....I HAVE RECEIVED WORD THAT THE ONE WE SEEK HAS BEEN SEEN IN YOUR TERRITORY.... ...HOW IS IT THAT YOU HAVE NOT BROUGHT HIM TO ME?

WE--WE HAVE NOT SEEN THE ONE WHO BEARS THE STAR--

BUT ON SEVERAL OCCASIONS WE HAVE SEEN ONE WHO IS MUCH LIKE HIM IN DESCRIPTION.... HE IS CALLED FONE BONE....

WE FIRST SAW HIM ON THE WESTERN RIDGE-- ON THE DRAGONS' STAIR-- WE HAVE SEEN THIS NEW CREATURE TWICE MORE IN THE VALLEY NEAR THE WATERFALL....

DID YOU THINK THIS WAS INSIGNIFICANT? WHY DID YOU NOT CAPTURE THE CREATURE AND BRING IT TO THE COUNCIL?

...HE BEARS NO STAR...

WE TRIED TO CAPTURE HIM, MASTER....BUT HE IS CHARMED! HE IS UNDER THE PROTECTION OF THE GREAT RED DRAGON!

WE TRIED TO SPY.... BUT THE DRAGON TREADS A WIDE CIRCLE AROUND HIM...

THE CREATURE IS ON A SMALL FARM NEAR THE HOT SPRINGS... HE STAYS WITH THE OLD COW WOMAN ...MOTHER BEN.....

...., THESE ARE GRAVE TIDINGS....IT WOULD NOT BE WELL FOR THE DRAGON TO LEARN OF OUR PLANS....

....IF WE MUST RISK A CONFRONTATION..... WE MUST DO IT NOW... WHILE THE DRAGON'S SUSPICIONS SLEEP....

KINGDOK...PREPARE TWO WAR PARTIES.....TAKE A THOUSAND WARRIORS IN EACH....

WITH THE FIRST.... SCOUR THE COUNTRYSIDE... SEARCH THE ROAD AND THE LANDS BEYOND THE WATERFALL.... FIND THE ONE WHO BEARS THE STAR.....

....IF THE DRAGON IS STILL WATCHING....THIS ACTIVITY WILL DRAW HIM OFF...LEAVING THE OLD COW WOMAN UNGUARDED.....

SEND THE SECOND PARTY TO THE FARMHOUSE .... DESTROY IT....... ...KILL THE NEW CREATURE...

LET US HOPE THAT THE DEATH OF THIS FONE BONE WILL CAUSE THE DRAGON TO LEAVE THE VALLEY AND RETURN TO DEREN GARD....

...GO NOW.... WE ATTACK TONIGHT!

FONE BONE! I HAD THE **DREAM** AGAIN! THE RAT CREATURES WERE **ATTACKING!**

IT'S NO DREAM! *IT'S* HAPPENING!

NO --

THE RAT CREATURES HAVE SURROUNDED TH' FARM!! *HURRY!* GRAN'MA'S WAITING FOR US *DOWNSTAIRS!*

HOW MANY ARE THERE?

DON'T KNOW... HERE, BONE. HOLD THIS!

OH, MAN!

I CAN HEAR 'EM MOVIN' **AROUND** OUT THERE!

THORN, DEAR... BRING ME A POKER FROM THE FIREPLACE -- AND YOU BETTER PUT SOME **SHOES** ON...

DO YOU HAVE A **PLAN**, GRAN'MA?

I HAVE AN IDEA THAT MIGHT WORK.

OKAY, CHILDREN! LISTEN CLOSELY! THIS IS WHAT WE'RE GOING TO DO...

-- WHEN I SAY RUN... ...YOU **RUN!** GOT THAT?

WHAT?!

THAT'S YOUR **PLAN**? RUN **WHERE**?

READY?

HERE WE GO!

CRASSSH

SPLINTER

K-KRRK-K-K

OKAY, KIDS! RUN!

CRUNCH

UH . . .

NOW, BONE!

WE CAN'T JUST **LEAVE** YOU HERE!

COME **ON,** FONE BONE!

DON'T WORRY ABOUT **ME**--

BIF!

SPLAT!

I FOUGHT TH' RATS BACK IN TH' **BIG** WAR!

OHMYGOSH

THUD. THUD. WAK!

OHMYGOSH

OHMYGOSH

GET UP! GET UP!

WHAT
HAPPENED?

WHY
ARE WE
STOPPING?

Shh! WE HAVE
TO GO BACK!
GRAN'MA
NEEDS OUR
HELP!

NOW
YOU'RE
WORRIED
ABOUT
GRAN'MA?!

THERE'S TOO
MANY! SHE
DIDN'T KNOW
THE WOODS
WERE FULL OF
MONSTERS!

AAAAH!

CREEEAK

IT **IS** YOU! THANK **GOODNESS** I'VE **FOUND** YOU!!

YA **MEAN** IT, PHONEY? YOU'RE **HAPPY** TO SEE ME?

DARN RIGHT!! FONE BONE WOULDN'T LET ME **LEAVE** THIS STUPID VALLEY UNLESS I **FOUND** YOU FIRST!

AW, SHUCKS-- IT'S GOOD TO SEE YOU, **TOO**, CUZ!

THIS CALLS FOR A **TOAST!** LET ME BUY YOU A **DRINK**, OL' **BUDDY!**

OKAY BY **ME**, OL' **PAL!**

HERE'S TO GOIN' **HOME!**

TO BONEVILLE!

CLINK

TO BONEVILLE!

GLUG! GLUG!

AHH!

SMEK SMEK

WHADDYA SAY WE HAVE ANOTHER ROUND ON **YOU**, OL' FRIEND!

SURE! WHY **NOT?** I GOT A FEELIN' MY **LUCK'S** ABOUT TO **CHANGE!** --GUESS WHERE FONE BONE IS **RIGHT NOW!** HE'S WITH **GRAN'MA BEN!** YOU KNOW-- TH' OLD LADY THAT RACES **COWS!**

AH! YOU'RE IN TOWN FOR TH' **COW RACE!** ME TOO! THERE'S GONNA BE SOME HEAVY **BETTIN'** GOIN' ON!

SO I'VE HEARD!

IS ANYBODY DOIN' TH' **BOOKMAKIN'**?

NOT YET. . . BUT FROM WHAT I'VE PICKED UP - - YOUR FRIEND **GRAN'MA** IS TH' **ODDS-ON** FAVORITE!

GREAT! PERFECT! HOW MUCH TIME DO WE HAVE?

ONE WEEK.

EXCELLENT! I GOT AN **IDEA** THAT'LL MAKE US A **LOTTA** MONEY!

UH, OH! I HOPE THIS ISN'T GONNA BE ONE OF THOSE **SILLY** IDEAS YOU USED TO PULL BACK IN **BONEVILLE!**

WHAT?! WHAT ARE YOU **TALKIN'** ABOUT? **WHAT** SILLY IDEAS?!

REMEMBER TH' **FIRST** TIME YOU GOT US RUN OUT OF TOWN? YOU OPENED UP A CHAIN OF FRANCHISES - - **BONE ENVIRONMENTAL:** NUCLEAR REACTOR AND ENDLESS SALAD BARS!

THAT WASN'T A **SILLY** IDEA! TH' **LETTUCE** WOULDN'T SPOIL FOR **DECADES!**

WELL, IT WAS **PRETTY** SILLY!

OH, YEAH, YOU'RE A **BRILLIANT** JUDGE!

NOW- - WHERE ARE WE GONNA FIND A **COW SUIT?**

WHAT? I GET TO WEAR A COW SUIT?! COOL! HAVE ANOTHER **BEER,** PARTNER!

KEEP IT **DOWN**, YOU CORN HEAD! I DON'T WANT ANYBODY TO KNOW WE'RE **TOGETHER!**

oh! RIGHT! **GOTCHA!**

OH, NO! NOT **ANOTHER** ONE*!!* YOU BETTER BE ABLE TO **PAY** FOR THOSE BEERS, SHORTY!

DON'T WORRY! I'LL PRETEND I DON'T KNOW YOU . . . HUM TE DUM

THAT'S **FIVE MUGS** OF MY **BEST ALE!** YOU OWE ME **TWO EGGS**, AN' I WANT IT **NOW!**

RELAX, KING KONG! I'M **GOOD** FOR IT!

DOO, DOO!

JUST LIKE THIS **OTHER** IDIOT WAS **GOOD** FOR IT?!

OH, MY! LOOK AT ALL THESE DIRTY GLASSES!

I'VE HAD IT UP TO **HERE** WITH YOU DRIFTERS COMIN' INTO TOWN FOR TH' FESTIVAL -- TRYIN' TO GET **BEER** ON **CREDIT!**

QUIT BREATHIN' IN MY **CUP!**

IT'S **MY** CUP UNTIL YOU PAY ME THE **TWO EGGS** YOU OWE ME!!

JEEZ! WHAT A **HOTHEAD! HERE!** TAKE IT!

WHAT'S THIS?

TWO **EGGS**, PAL! WHAT? DID TH' PRICE GO UP?

OKAY, SHORTY! **GET** IN TH' KITCHEN! YOU CAN **WORK** OFF YER BAR TAB...

WH - - ?

HEY!

NOBODY MUTILATES A **MINT NOTE** AROUND **ME** AN' LIVES TO **TELL** ABOUT IT! **SAY YER PRAYERS, CHUCKLES!**

THEY DON'T **USE** MONEY HERE, CUZ! THEY'VE NEVER EVEN **SEEN** IT BEFORE!

COME AGAIN?

THEY TRADE **GOODS** AND **SERVICES**. IT'S A **BARTER SYSTEM!**

CHUCKLES WANTS **REAL EGGS!**

YOUR BUTT IS **MINE**, BALDY!

SMILEY - - **WHY** DID YOU KEEP GIVING ME BEER? YOU **KNOW** I DON'T CARRY **DAIRY PRODUCTS!!**

UH, OH! LOOKS LIKE I MISSED SOME OF THOSE DIRTY GLASSES!

THEY'RE CIRCLING US!

WHAT DO YOU WANT?!

SSSSSS---- ✳

WE WANT THE SMALL CREATURE.....

YOU CAN'T HAVE HIM!

GO AWAY!

GIVE IT TO US...

....DEFIANCE WILL NOT BE TOLERATED...... .....ONCE **WE** RETURN ORDER TO THE VALLEY......

STAY BACK!

SNIFF! SNIFF!

WAIT A MINUTE! WAIT A MINUTE!

DO YOU **SMELL** THAT?!

IT'S BRIMSTONE! IT'S THE **DRAGON!** HE'S **HERE!**

OH, NO.

RELAX, THORN! EVERYTHING'S GONNA BE **OKAY!**

FONE BONE! WHAT ARE YOU DOING?!

I KNOW **YOU** DON'T BELIEVE IN DRAGONS, BUT **THESE GUYS** DO! WATCH **THIS!**

OKAY, FELLAS! PARTY'S **OVER**! BREAK IT UP! **LET'S GO**! TH' DRAGON'LL BE HERE **ANY MINUTE** NOW, AN' YOU DON'T WANNA **BE** HERE WHEN HE SHOWS UP!

JUST THE **SIGHT** OF TH' DRAGON SENDS THESE GUYS INTO A **PANIC**! THEY RUN LIKE THEIR **FUR'S** ON FIRE!

ARE YOU STILL **HERE**? **GO ON**! **SHOO**!

I SMELL NOTHING...

WHAT ARE YOU **TALKIN'** ABOUT? YOU DON'T SMELL BRIMSTONE?

SSSSSS

NO.

SNIFF! SNIFF! **THAT'S** WEIRD! I DON'T SMELL IT ANYMORE, EITHER!

LOOK OUT!

AARR

OOF!

CHUNK

WHY, LOOK, TED. IT'S A MEETING OF THE NEW COMMUNITY LEADERS.

OOH! A TOWN **MEETING!** DOES WE GITS TA **VOTE?** I JES **LOVES** TA VOTE!

HISSS! STAY BACK, WORM!

OUR NUMBERS ARE TOO GREAT!

EVEN FOR YOU!

FUNNY YOU SHOULD MENTION THAT-- HOW MANY WARRIORS **DO** YOU HAVE BETWEEN HERE AND THE **WATERFALL?** A THOUSAND? **TWO THOUSAND?**

HIYA, BONES! HEY, THORNY! C'MON OVER HERE!

SSSSSS

I **BELIEVE** THIS VIOLATES OUR AGREEMENT...

YOU WOULD NOT BE SO BOLD IF **KINGDOK** WERE HERE!

YOU RUN AND TELL KINGDOK THAT I'M **WATCHIN'** HIM!

HE **DID** IT! **YES!** I **TOLD** YOU THERE WAS A DRAGON! I **TOLD** YOU!

MR. DRAGON...

MM?

... THE RAT CREATURES ATTACKED OUR FARM — —

WE LEFT MY GRANDMOTHER THERE ALONE!

CLIMB ON MY BACK.

C'MON, FONE BONE!

OHMYGOSH

HOLD TIGHT!

HURRY!

STOP! STOP! LOOK!

WE'RE TOO LATE - -

...THEY MIGHT BE **WATCHING!**

I **DON'T CARE!!**

GRAN'MA!

I'LL GO **WITH** YA, **THORNY!** WAIT FOR **ME!**

C'MON!

GRAN'MA? CAN YOU HEAR ME?

GRAN'MA BEN! WHERE ARE YOU?

CRASH *TINKLE!*

THORN?
IS THAT
YOU, DEAR?

OH, GOOD!
YOU'RE SAFE!

CRUNCH!
TINK!

GRAN'MA--!

ARE YOU
ALL
RIGHT?

OF COURSE I AM, DEAR!
I FOUGHT TH' RATS BACK
IN TH' BIG WAR! BESIDES,
I WASN'T REALLY IN DANGER...

... WHEN YOU AN' BONE LEFT TH'
HOUSE, ALL TH' FIGHT WENT OUT
OF 'EM! I WAS MUCH MORE
WORRIED ABOUT YOU!

WE ALMOST GOT CAUGHT,
BUT THE DRAGON SAVED US!

A **REAL** DRAGON, GRAN'MA!

LOOK!

I CAN SEE.

HELLO, DRAGON.

HELLO, ROSE.

IT'S BEEN A WHILE.

YEP.

WELL . . . LOOKS LIKE EVERYTHING'S UNDER CONTROL HERE. GUESS I'LL BE GOIN'.

YEP.

C'MON, TED.

GRAN'MA! WHAT ARE YOU DOING?! THE DRAGON JUST SAVED OUR LIVES!

NOT NOW, THORN. MR. BONE FROM BONEVILLE AN' I HAVE TO HAVE A LITTLE CHAT!

AND **YOU** HAVE A LOT OF THINGS TO DO BEFORE WE LEAVE FOR TH' **SPRING FAIR**!

THE **FAIR**?! YOU'RE NOT STILL WORRIED ABOUT YOUR **COW RACE**?!

WHAT ABOUT **PHONEY BONE** AN' **SMILEY**? WE HAVE TO **FIND** THEM!

BONE AND I WILL HITCH UP TH' CART. **YOU** BE A SWEETHEART AND PUT OUT TH' **FIRE** ON TH' **ROOF**!

SHE'S NOT EVEN **LISTENING** TO US! CAN YOU **BELIEVE** SHE WANTS TO GO TO TH' **FAIR**?!

ARE YOU **KIDDING**? I STILL CAN'T GET OVER TH' FACT THAT SHE HAS A **FIRST NAME**!

DEAR . . . I'M NOT A **COMPLETE** NINCOMPOOP! WE'LL BE **SAFER** IN TOWN! **AND**, WITH ANY LUCK, WE'LL BE ABLE TO FIND HIS **COUSINS**!

BUT – –

PLEASE, THORN! WE **HAVE** TO **GO**! WE DON'T KNOW IF THEY'RE **SAFE**!

YOU'RE RIGHT! I'LL TAKE CARE OF THE ROOF!

WE PACKED EVERYTHING LAST NIGHT, SO TH' LUGGAGE IS ALREADY OUT IN TH' BARN. COME JOIN US WHEN YOU GET DONE.

C'MON, BONE!

GRAN'MA? WHAT **WAS** THAT WITH YOU AN' TH' DRAGON? DO YOU GUYS **KNOW** EACH OTHER?

I'LL ASK TH' QUESTIONS! I WANNA KNOW WHY THOSE MONSTERS WERE AFTER **YOU** . . . AN' I WANT TH' **TRUTH**!

I HAVE **NO** IDEA! **HONEST**! I'VE NEVER DONE **ANYTHING** TO THEM!

WHAT ABOUT THAT SHIFTY **COUSIN** OF YOURS? YOU THINK **PHONEY BONE** MIGHT'VE HAD SOME DEALIN'S WITH 'EM?

NO, MA'M! WE DON'T **HAVE** RAT CREATURES BACK WHERE WE COME FROM!

IN FACT, WE NEVER EVEN **HEARD** OF RAT CREATURES BEFORE WE GOT RUN OUT OF BONEVILLE!

WELL, ACTUALLY, **I** WASN'T RUN OUTTA BONEVILLE -- **PHONEY** WAS! SMILEY AN' I JUST HELPED HIM GET AWAY!

WHAT'D HE **DO?**

PHONEY DECIDED HE WAS GONNA RUN FOR **MAYOR!** HIS CAMPAIGN SLOGAN WAS: "AN' I'VE GOT TH' **MONEY** TO **DO** IT, TOO!"

SO TH' BONES RAN HIM OUTTA TOWN FOR **THAT,** HUH? WELL, **GOOD** FOR THEM!

NO. ANYBODY CAN RUN FOR MAYOR. EVEN **PHONEY!**

THAT GREEDY, LITTLE **LOUDMOUTH?** NOT IN MY TOWN HE COULDN'T!

WELL, HE CAN IN BONEVILLE. **ANYWAY,** HE WANTED TO MAKE THE **OFFICIAL** ANNOUNCEMENT A BIG **SOCIAL EVENT,** SO HE DECIDED TO THROW A PICNIC DOWN ON TH' BANKS OF TH' **ROLLING BONE** RIVER . . .

THERE'S A **BEAUTIFUL** PARK THERE WITH GREEN, SLOPING LAWNS THAT STRETCH TO THE EDGE OF TH' WATER. IT'S JUST FAR ENOUGH AWAY FROM TH' **HUSTLE** AN' **BUSTLE** OF DOWNTOWN BONEVILLE THAT THERE WOULDN'T BE ANY **DISTRACTIONS!**

PHONEY INVITED **EVERYBODY** IN TOWN -- AN' HE PROMISED **FREE FOOD** FOR ANYONE WHO SHOWED UP! PRETTY SOON, TH' **PICNIC** WAS TH' **TALK** OF **BONEVILLE!**

THEN TH' BIG DAY ARRIVED, AN' TH' **WHOLE TOWN** TURNED OUT! TH' KIDS WERE PLAYIN' UNDER TH' TREES, AN' THE WOMEN WORE SUNBONNETS AN' FANCY DRESSES! THE PICNIC WAS OFF TO A **PERFECT START!**

THERE'S A **STATUE** IN TH' PARK OF BONEVILLE'S **FOUNDER** -- "BIG" JOHNSON BONE -- AN' SINCE MY COUSINS AN' I ARE **DESCENDANTS** OF HIS, PHONEY WANTED TO MAKE HIS ANNOUNCEMENT IN FRONT OF TH' STATUE.

. . . AND JUST TO **ADD** TO TH' FESTIVITIES, PHONEY HAD A **50** ft. **BALLOON** MADE OF HIMSELF! TH' BALLOON WAS TIED TO OL' "BIG" JOHNSON!

FASTEN THAT END THERE, WOULD YOU, BONE?

EVERYTHING WAS GOIN' **GREAT!** FOLKS WERE LISTENIN' TO TH' **FIREHOUSE** BAND AN' ENJOYIN' TH' SUNSHINE! TH' FOOD WAS PASSED OUT AN' THERE WERE PLENTY OF PRUNE **TARTS** FOR **EVERYONE!**

PRUNE TARTS?

YEAH. YOU KNOW PHONEY. HE GOT A GOOD DEAL ON SOME PRUNES FROM A DISCOUNT **PRUNE BROKER!**

OF COURSE!

SO ANYWAY, HE MAKES THE **ANNOUNCEMENT**, RIGHT? HE GETS UP AND DECLARES HIS CANDIDACY FOR MAYOR OF BONEVILLE!

I STILL THINK **THAT'S** WHEN THEY SHOULD'VE RUN HIM OUT!

THAT'S WHEN A GUST OF WIND CAME OFF TH' RIVER AND PULLED TH' **BALLOON** LOOSE! THE STATUE CAME OFF ITS **BASE** AN' WAS DANGLIN' OFF TH' BALLOON'S **ANKLE**! ALL OF A **SUDDEN**, THIS GIANT, INFLATABLE PHONEY BONE STARTED MOVING TOWARD THE **CROWD**!

OH, MY!

YEAH, IT WAS **AMAZING**! MY FIRST-GRADE TEACHER, **MISS CRAB-BONE**, WAS THE FIRST TO **PANIC**! SHE STARTED SCREAMING AND RUNNING BACK AN' FORTH! THE BALLOON CHASED HER INTO TH' **RIVER** BEFORE SMILEY AND I COULD LET THE **AIR** OUT OF IT!

... IT WAS **AWFUL**! EVERYONE WAS **STUNNED**! AT FIRST NOBODY MOVED! THEY JUST **SAT** THERE WITH THIS LOOK OF **HORROR** ON THEIR FACES!

AN' **THAT'S** WHEN THEY RAN YOU OUTTA TOWN.

NO. THAT'S WHEN TH' **BAD PRUNES** KICKED IN...

HEY, **SMILEY!** TAKE THAT TUB OF GLASSES BACK TO YOUR BUDDY! WE'RE OUT OF **MUGS** AGAIN!

YES, **SIR**, MISTER DOWN!

HEY, THERE, PHONEY! LUCIUS SAYS YA GOTTA **WASH** THESE, **PRONTO!** WE GOT A LOT OF **THIRSTY CUSTOMERS** OUT FRONT!

OF COURSE, I MAKE **SURE** EVERYBODY GETS A **NEW, CLEAN MUG** WITH EACH DRINK!

YEAH. I NOTICED.

CLUNK

...I JUST WANT YOU TO **KNOW**... I'VE BEEN **WORKING** ON **THE PLAN!** I BEEN SPREADIN' **RUMORS** ALL DAY THAT **GRAN'MA BEN** IS **TOO OLD** TO WIN TH' RACE THIS YEAR!

IS ANYBODY **BUYIN'** IT?

I'M TH' **BARTENDER!** THEY **GOTTA** BELIEVE ME!

THIS IS **TOO** **EASY!** WE'LL COVER ALL TH' **BETS,** AND THEN WHEN GRAN'MA **WINS,** WE'LL BE **RICH!**

OF COURSE, WHEN GRAN'MA GETS INTO **TOWN,** EVERYBODY'S GONNA **SEE** SHE'S PERFECTLY FIT!

I'VE GOT THAT COVERED WITH **PHASE TWO:**

THE MYSTERY COW!

A **COW** THAT WE'LL **BUILD UP** IN EVERYBODY'S IMAGINATION THAT **CAN'T BE BEAT!**

WAIT! IS **THAT** TH' PART WHERE I GET TO WEAR TH' **COW SUIT**?! OH, **JOY!**

YEAH, **THAT'S** TH' PART!' BUT YOU'RE GONNA **THROW** TH' RACE! REMEMBER! WE **WANT** GRAN'MA BEN TO WIN!

WELL, **NATURALLY,** I'M LOOKING FORWARD TO WEARIN' A **COW SUIT** -- BUT WHAT DO **YOU** GET OUT OF IT? AFTER **ALL,** THE LOCALS DON'T USE **MONEY!** THEY TRADE **GOODS 'N' SERVICES!**

IT **DOES** SOUR MY PLANS FOR AMASSING A **HUGE** FORTUNE AND RETURNING TO BONEVILLE IN **TRIUMPH**... **STILL,** THE PLAY IS TH' THING!

IF ALL THESE YOKELS **HAVE** ARE **POULTRY PRODUCTS,** THEN I'LL

TAKE IT!!

BESIDES, I HAVE A **HANKERIN'** TO TAKE TH' PROPRIETOR OF THIS FINE ESTABLISHMENT TO TH' **CLEANERS.'** YOU **WITH** ME?

SURE.' IT DOESN'T MAKE ANY DIFFERENCE TO **ME.'** BUT THEN ... NOT MUCH **DOES.'**

GOOD. NOW GET BACK OUT THERE AND KEEP SPREADIN' **RUMORS.'**

AN' QUIT BRINGIN' ME DIRTY DISHES TO WASH!

PHONCIBLE P. BONE ..... AT **LAST** I HAVE FOUND YOU .....

WHO, **ME?** HOW DO YOU **KNOW** MY NAME?

...YOU SHOULD BE GRATEFUL INDEED THAT YOUR FRIENDS INTERFERED ON YOUR BEHALF LAST NIGHT.... I AM FORCED TO USE MUCH MORE SUBTLE METHODS OF CONTACTING YOU....

WHAT TH' **HECK** ARE YOU **TALKIN'** ABOUT?

..... YOUR COUSIN FONE BONE HAS AWAKENED THE GREAT RED DRAGON .... FOR THIS ... ... I WILL **KILL** HIM .....

SORRY, CUZ, BUT
LUCIUS SAYS YOU
GOTTA WASH
THESE!

UH, OH.

YES. WE SAW THEM. MAY WE PASS?

OH, YES, MA'M! COME AROUND TH' END, HERE!

H'LO, MISS THORN!

HELLO, JON.

GOOD LUCK WITH TH' BIG **RACE**, **GRAN'MA!** EVERYONE'S **BETTIN'** ON YA!

THANK YOU, DEAR!

THORN?

YES, FONE BONE?

I WANT TO THANK YOU FOR STICKIN' WITH ME LAST NIGHT . . . I DON'T KNOW WHY THOSE RAT CREATURES WERE **AFTER** ME – – BUT THEY WOULD'VE **GOT** ME FOR **SURE** IF YOU HADN'T **STOOD UP** TO 'EM!

OF **COURSE** WE STUCK TOGETHER! WE'RE **FRIENDS**, AREN'T WE?

HURRY UP, NOW, KIDS! WE'RE HERE!

WELL, WELL... IT'S ABOUT **TIME!**

HELLO, LUCIUS!

HOW YA DOIN', ROSIE? WAS TH' **ROAD** SAFE? I WAS **WORRIED** ABOUT YA!

TH' ROAD WAS CLEAR... EXCEPT FOR YOUR **ROADBLOCK!**

OH! I GOT SOMETHIN' FOR YA! HERE! I BEEN SAVIN' IT IN MY POCKET ALL DAY!

OH, AREN'T YOU SWEET!

...WELLL..... I HAD A LITTLE EXTRA **TIME** ON MY HANDS THIS MORNING...

...I GOT A COUPLE OF **DEADBEATS** INSIDE TAKIN' CARE OF TH' **CUSTOMERS --** IN FACT, THEY LOOK A **LOT** LIKE THIS LITTLE FELLA YOU GOT HERE.

THEY **DO?!**

YO, FONE BONE!

SMILEY BONE!

YAY! MY LITTLE PAL IS **SAFE!**

OH, MY **GOSH!** I WAS SO **WORRIED** ABOUT YOU!

AW, HECK, **I** CAN TAKE CARE OF MYSELF! I'M **BIG!** BUT YOU'RE **SMALL,** AN' YOU DIDN'T HAVE ANYBODY TO LOOK **AFTER** YOU!

HOLD ME OUT, SO I CAN TAKE A **LOOK** AT YOU!

DO I LOOK GOOD?

YOU LOOK **GOOD,** MAN!

AN ODE TO QUICHE

A POEM BY JEFF SMITH
WITH COLOR BY TOM GAADT

An Ode to Quiche

I weesh, I weesh I had a quiche.
A flakey-wakey, puffy quiche.
   A delicious quiche all golden brown.
A custard pie with a pastry crown.

I'd prepare the filling with loving care,
and whip the eggs as light as air.
I ask myself how hungry I am --
hungry enough to add some ham!

The thing that turns this dream to bad
is the constant noise from my comrade.
Words come out, but don't make sense.
A hater of pastry, he seems so dense.

His jaws go up, his jaws go down,
but what comes out is A bossy sound.
He screams, he rants, he always yells,
He stinks, he stunks, he really smells.

He likes his meat raw, or baked in a stew,
but does that mean that I have to, too?!
The world is filled with wonderful flavors,
a smorgasbord for us to savor.

Would he prefer cake?
or go jump in the lake?
Who says it's a law
That we eat our meat raw?

I weesh, I weesh I had some Quiche,
but all I have is that Nin-com-peesh.
If only his taste buds would mature.
What a stupid, stupid Rat Creature.

PINUP ART

MOMENTS FROM *OUT FROM BONEVILLE*

The Adventure Begins

Crossing the Dragon's Stair

Fone Bone Meets Thorn

Boneville? What's Boneville?

Find the One Who Bears the Star

Hello, Rose

Together Again

TRIBUTE GALLERY

Kate Beaton
The Princess and the Pony

Jeffrey Brown
Jedi Academy

James Burks
Bird & Squirrel

Frank Cammuso
Knights of the Lunch Table

Nathan Fox
Dogs of War

Jimmy Gownley
The Dumbest Idea Ever

Kazu Kibuishi
Amulet

Mike Maihack
Cleopatra in Space

Scott Morse
Magic Pickle

Jake Parker
Missile Mouse

Dav Pilkey
Captain Underpants

Greg Ruth
The Lost Boy

Dan Santat
Sidekicks

Raina Telgemeier
Sisters

Doug TenNapel
NNEWTS

Craig Thompson
Space Dumplins

Kate Beaton

Jeffrey Brown

Frank Cammuso

Nathan Fox

Jimmy Gownley

Kazu Kibuishi

Mike Maihack

Scott Morse

Jake Parker

Dav Pilkey

Greg Ruth

Dan Santat

Raina Telgemeier

Doug TenNapel

The BONE saga continues in

Here's a preview!

HELLO, WE'D LIKE TO BUY A COUPLE OF YOUR COMBS!

STEP RIGHT OVER HERE, MISS!

MY NAME'S TOM. WHAT'S YOURS?

THORN. DO YOU HAVE ANYTHING FROM SOUTH VALLEY?

SURE **DO!** GOT COMBS FROM SOUTH VALLEY **AND** FROM **PAWA!** BUT A SWEET LITTLE THING LIKE **YOU** PROB'LY WANTS HONEY FROM **ATHEIA!**

HERE! JUST **SMELL** IT! NOTHIN' IN THE WHOLE **VALLEY** COMPARES TO IT -- . . . EXCEPT MAYBE **YOU** . . .

IT DOES SMELL NICE.

WANNA TAKE A **WHIFF,** LITTLE FELLA? YOU OUGHTA APPRECIATE IT WITH A NOSE LIKE **THAT!**

HEY!

WHAT **IS** HE ANYWAY? DOES HE **ALWAYS** FOLLOW YOU AROUND?

HE'S MY FRIEND. AND WE CAN **BOTH** SMELL THE HONEY JUST FINE. WE'LL TAKE TWO COMBS.

IT'S NOT **THAT** BIG.

THAT'S ENOUGH! YOU CAN'T TALK TO MY FRIEND THAT WAY!

COME ON, FONE BONE!

WHAT WERE YOU THINKING? I'VE NEVER SEEN YOU ACT THAT WAY BEFORE!

HE STARTED IT WITH THAT CRACK ABOUT MY NOSE!

I DON'T CARE WHO STARTED IT! IT WAS EMBARRASSING!

BUT --

WHEN YOU CAN WALK AROUND THE FAIR WITHOUT GETTING INTO A FIGHT -- COME FIND ME! UNTIL THEN, I'D RATHER BE BY MYSELF!

HONEY!

THIS IS **GREAT!** I'LL GET THORN SOME HONEY **MYSELF!**

HOW HARD CAN IT BE? I JUST NEED SOME **GREEN GRASS** THAT'LL **SMOKE REAL GOOD** WHEN I LIGHT IT . . .

. . . THEN I'LL **WAVE** TH' SMOKE IN FRONT OF TH' HIVE UNTIL TH' BEES FALL **ASLEEP!**

THIS IS GONNA BE LIKE TAKING **CANDY** FROM A **BABY!**

NOW TO JUST **SHIMMY** UP TH' TREE!

Don't miss any of the BONE books!

OUT FROM BONEVILLE

THE GREAT COW RACE

EYES OF THE STORM

THE DRAGONSLAYER

ROCK JAW
Master of the Eastern Border

OLD MAN'S CAVE

GHOST CIRCLES

TREASURE HUNTERS

CROWN OF HORNS

ROSE

TALL TALES

HANDBOOK

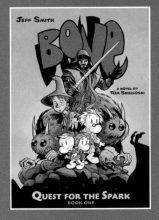

QUEST FOR THE SPARK
BOOK ONE

QUEST FOR THE SPARK
BOOK TWO

QUEST FOR THE SPARK
BOOK THREE

ABOUT THE AUTHOR

JEFF SMITH was born and raised in the American Midwest and learned about cartooning from comic strips, comic books, and watching animated shorts on TV. After four years of drawing comic strips for The Ohio State University's student newspaper and cofounding Character Builders animation studio in 1986, Smith launched the comic book BONE in 1991. As BONE's popularity grew, he became known as a cofounder of the self-publishing movement of the 1990s and an early adopter of the graphic novel format. Smith was the subject of a 2009 documentary called *The Cartoonist: Jeff Smith, BONE, and the Changing Face of Comics.* Today, BONE is available in more than 20 languages, and there are millions of copies in print. Between BONE and other comics projects, Smith spends much of his time on the international guest circuit promoting comics and the art of graphic novels. Visit him online at www.boneville.com.

Dreaming of Harvestar